All children have a great ambition to read to themselves...

and a sense of achievement when they can do so. The **read it yourself** *series has been devised to satisfy their ambition. Since many children learn from the Ladybird Key Words Reading Scheme, these stories have been based to a large extent on the Key Words List, and the tales chosen are those with which children are likely to be familiar.*

The series can of course be used as supplementary reading for any reading scheme.

Gingerbread Man *is intended for children reading up to Book 4c of the Ladybird Reading Scheme. The following words are additional to the vocabulary used at that level –*

gingerbread, fox, old, woman, oven, soon, cooked, out, of, can't, runs, eat, swim, tail, feet, back, again, head, nose, SNAP, gulp, went

A list of other titles at the same level will be found on the back cover.

© LADYBIRD BOOKS LTD MCMLXXVII

All rights reserved. No part of this publication may be reproduced, stored in a retrieval system, or transmitted in any form or by any means, electronic, mechanical, photocopying, recording or otherwise, without the prior consent of the copyright owner.

Gingerbread Man

by Fran Hunia
illustrated by Brian Price Thomas

Ladybird Books Loughborough

A little old man

and a little old woman

have a house on a farm.

Two children come to help

on the farm.

The little old woman says
to the children,
"I want to make you
some good things for tea.
Do you want a big cake
or a gingerbread man?"

"We like gingerbread,"
say the children.
"Please make us
a gingerbread man."

The little old woman
makes a gingerbread man.

She puts him in the oven
and then she gets on
with her work.

9

Soon the gingerbread man
is cooked. The little old woman
gets him out of the oven.

"What a good gingerbread man,"
she says. "The children can have him
for tea."

11

The gingerbread man looks up.

"No, no, they can't," he says.

"No one will have me for tea."

He jumps down and runs off.

"Stop, stop,"
says the little old woman.

"No, I will not stop,
and you can't get me,"
says the gingerbread man,
and he runs out of the house.

13

The little old man is at work on the farm.

He sees the gingerbread man.
"Stop, little gingerbread man," he says.
"The children want to have you for tea."

"No, no," says the gingerbread man.

"I will not stop for you.

The little old woman can't get me,

and you can't get me.

No one will have me for tea."

The gingerbread man runs on.

17

The children see

the gingerbread man.

"Stop, little gingerbread man,"

they say. "We want to have you

for tea."

"No, no," says the gingerbread man.

"I will not stop for you.

The little old woman can't get me,

the little old man can't get me,

and you can't get me.

No one will have me for tea."

He runs on.

A horse sees the gingerbread man.
"Stop, little gingerbread man,"
he says. "Let me have you
for my tea."

"No, no," says the gingerbread man.

"I will not stop for you.

The little old woman can't get me,

the little old man can't get me,

the children can't get me,

and you can't get me.

No one will have me for tea."

He runs on.

25

A cow sees the gingerbread man.

"Stop, little gingerbread man,"

she says. "I want

to have you for my tea."

"No, no," says the gingerbread man.

"I will not stop for you.

The little old woman can't get me,

the little old man can't get me,

the children can't get me,

the horse can't get me,

and you can't get me.

No one will have me for tea."

He runs on.

29

A dog sees the gingerbread man.

"Stop, little gingerbread man,"

he says. "Let me eat you up

for tea."

"No, no," says the gingerbread man.

"I will not stop for you.

The little old woman can't get me,

the little old man can't get me,

the children can't get me,

the horse can't get me,

the cow can't get me,

and you can't get me.

No one will have me for tea."

He runs on.

33

A cat sees the gingerbread man.

"Stop, little gingerbread man," says the cat. "I want to eat you up."

"No, no," says the gingerbread man.

"I will not stop for you.

The little old woman can't get me,

the little old man can't get me,

the children can't get me,

the horse can't get me,

the cow can't get me,

the dog can't get me,

and you can't get me.

No one will have me for tea."

He runs on.

37

The gingerbread man comes
to some water.
"What can I do?" he says.
"There is no boat here,
and I can't swim.
The cat and the dog and the cow
and the horse and the children
and the little old man
and the little old woman.
all want to eat me,
and I can't get away."

39

A fox comes up.

"Let me help you," he says.

"I can swim into the water
with you on my tail.
There will be no danger.
Come on. Jump on my tail."

41

The gingerbread man thanks the fox and jumps up on his tail.

Away they go into the water.

43

The gingerbread man can not
keep his feet out of the water.
"Please help me. My feet
are in the water," he says.

"Then get on my back,"
says the fox.

The gingerbread man
jumps on the fox's back,
and the fox swims on.

45

Soon the gingerbread man's feet
are in the water again.

"Please help me. My feet
are in the water," he says.

"Then get up on my head,"
says the fox.

The gingerbread man thanks
the fox and jumps up on his head.

The fox swims on.

47

Soon the gingerbread man's feet
are in the water again.

"Please help me. My feet
are in the water," he says.

"Then get up on my nose,"
says the fox.

The gingerbread man jumps up
on the fox's nose.

Then SNAP!
The fox eats him up
in one big gulp.

49

Then there was no gingerbread
man for the cat or the dog
or the cow or the horse.

or the children or the little old man

or the little old woman,

and they all went home again.